TWICE UPON A TIME

TWICE UPON A TIME

by Irwin Shapiro

illustrations by Adrienne Adams

Charles Scribner's Sons   New York

1 3 5 7 9 11 13 15 17 19 C/X 20 18 16 14 12 10 8 6 4 2

Printed in the United States of America
Library of Congress Catalog Card Number: 72–97116
SBN 684–13358–X

TWICE UPON A TIME

Once upon a time there was a writer of stories. His name was Rambling Richard, and he wandered all over the world.

He carried with him an ink pot and a bundle of paper. In his hat was stuck a goose quill pen.

Every morning he sat down and wrote a story. He dipped his goose quill pen in the ink pot, and began: "Once upon a time . . ."

He exchanged his stories for bread and cheese and a place to sleep. Sometimes — but not very often — he bought a new hat or a purple cloak with extra-large pockets.

As he walked along the dusty roads, he often sang a
song he had made up himself. It went like this:

> I've two eyes and ears,
>   Ten fingers and toes,
> I stand on my feet,
>   And follow my nose.
>
> I see what I see,
>   I know what I know,
> I hear what I hear,
>   And go where I go.
>
> I think what I think,
>   And say what I say,
> And sometimes I'm sad,
>   But mostly I'm gay.
>
> I am what I am,
>   You are what you are,
> The sun is the sun,
>   A star is a star.
>
> Sometimes it's day,
>   And sometimes it's night,
> Sometimes I'm wrong,
>   But mostly I'm right.

One day, following a crooked road, he came to the gate
of a city. It was the largest gate he had ever seen. Before it
stood two of the tallest soldiers he had ever seen. They were
holding the longest spears he had ever seen.

He said to one of the soldiers, "I am Rambling Richard,
the writer of stories. Stories funny and stories sad, for man
or woman, girl or lad. I am also a poet. Can you tell me what
place this is?"

"I can," answered the soldier in the deepest voice Rambling Richard had ever heard. "This is Gib-Gib."

"Thank you," said Rambling Richard. "And now, if you don't mind, I'll go into the city. I've been walking since morning, and it's a rather hot day."

"In Gib-Gib," said the soldier, "the days are twice as hot as anywhere else in the world."

"Is that so?" said Rambling Richard. "I hope the nights are cool."

"In Gib-Gib," said the soldier, "the nights are twice as cool as anywhere in the world."

"Well," said Rambling Richard, "I must say I like a milder climate."

"In Gib-Gib," said the soldier, "the climate is twice as mild as anywhere else in the world."

"Hmm," said Rambling Richard, and went into the city. The first thing he saw was a big sign. It said:

WELCOME TO GIB-GIB!
WATCH US GROW!
KING BIG-WIG THE GREAT

And everywhere in the city were other signs. They said:

BIGGER AND BIGGER!
FASTER AND FASTER!
HIGHER AND HIGHER!
MORE AND MORE!

As Rambling Richard looked at the signs, a man came walking down the street. He had a sad face full of wrinkles and crinkles.

"Hello," said Rambling Richard. "Friend, I am Rambling Richard, the writer of stories. Perhaps you can tell me something about Gib-Gib. You seem to have a great many signs."

"We have," said the sad man. "Twice as many as anywhere else in the world. We have twice as much or twice as many of everything in the world."

"You do?" said Rambling Richard.

The sad man sadly shook his head.

"No," he said, "not really. But we will if the king has his way. He wants two of anything anyone else has one of." And he sighed a long sigh.

"But why are you so sad?" asked Rambling Richard.

"The king wants everything twice as big, or twice as much, or twice as high, or twice as long," said the sad man. "And so we have to work twice as hard as anyone else in the world."

"Then why don't you stop?" said Rambling Richard.

"Ha!" said the sad man. "Look!" He pointed to a large, dark building. On it was a big sign that said: DOUBLE OR TROUBLE!

"Know what that is?" he said. "That's the jail. It's twice as big as any other jail in the world. That's where you land if you don't obey the king." The sad man sighed again.

"It isn't as if the king needed two of everything," he said. "Why does he need two palaces? Not even a king can live in two palaces at the same time. But there are worse things in Gib-Gib than two palaces. Come with me."

Taking Rambling Richard by the arm, he led him to a high mountain. Men were driving donkeys up the trails. The donkeys were loaded down with sacks of sticks, stones, earth, and rocks. On top of the mountain, men were working with shovels and wheelbarrows.

"What are they doing?" asked Rambling Richard.

"They're trying to make it higher," said the sad man. "The king wants a mountain twice as high as any other mountain in the world."

Suddenly there was a loud BOOM, and the top of the mountain fell off. Sticks and stones, earth and rocks, donkeys and men, shovels and wheelbarrows came tumbling down.

"See?" said the sad man. "That happens every day."

Then he led Rambling Richard to a field with a big, deep hole. Rambling Richard looked over the edge. Down in the hole were men, digging with picks and shovels.

"Know what they're doing?" said the sad man. "They're digging a hole twice as deep as any other hole in the world."

Suddenly there was a loud ZOOM, and one side of the hole fell in.

"That happens every day," said the sad man. And he looked sadder than ever.

"Perhaps one of my stories would cheer you up," said Rambling Richard. "I have stories funny and stories sad, for man or woman, girl or lad. I also have poems for a penny."

"I'll take a poem," said the sad man. "Do you have one about a midget?"

"No," said Rambling Richard. "But I have one about a mouse. A mouse is even smaller than a midget."

"Well . . ." said the sad man. "Could I see it?"

"Certainly," said Rambling Richard, and he showed the sad man the poem. It went like this:

> There once was a mouse,
> A tiny, tiny mouse,
>   He was so small
> A thimble was his house.

"All right. I'll take it," said the sad man.

After he had sold the sad man the poem, Rambling Richard looked for an inn. In return for a room, he gave the innkeeper a story. It was called, "How the World Shrank to the Size of a Pea and was Swallowed by an Oyster."

The next morning, Rambling Richard was up early. He sat down at the table to write a story. But before he could begin, he heard a knock on the door.

"Come in," he said, and there stood a man in a blue uniform.

"I am the king's messenger," he said. "I have a message for you from His Royal Majesty."

"And what is the message?" asked Rambling Richard.

"The king heard you were in the city," answered the messenger. "He wants you to write him a story about Gib-Gib. It must be twice as long as any story you have ever written. If it pleases the king, he will give you a bag of gold."

"What if my story does not please him?" asked Rambling Richard.

The king's messenger pointed out the window to the jail, and the sign that said: DOUBLE OR TROUBLE!

"Hmmm," said Rambling Richard.

And, bowing low, the king's messenger left the inn.

Rambling Richard thought for a few minutes. Dipping his goose quill pen in the ink pot, he began to write. Day after day he wrote, stopping only to eat or sleep. And every day he heard the top of the mountain falling off with a BOOM, and the hole falling in with a ZOOM.

At last the story was finished. Rambling Richard stuffed it into his pocket and walked to the king's palace. A servant took him to a big room where the king sat on his throne. The room was filled with soldiers, servants, and the king's uncles, cousins, and aunts.

"Rambling Richard," said the king, "are you ready to read your story?"

"I am," said Rambling Richard.

"Then do so," said the king.

Rambling Richard cleared his throat and began: "Once upon a time, in the kingdom of Gib-Gib . . ."

"Stop!" said the king, holding up his hand. "It may be all very well to say 'Once upon a time' in other lands. But in Gib-Gib everything is twice as big, and we have two of everything anyone else has one of. So your story must begin, 'Twice upon a time.'"

"Twice upon a time?" repeated Rambling Richard.

"Exactly," said the king.

Rambling Richard tried to speak, but he couldn't. He was laughing too hard.

"What's so funny?" said the king, frowning.

"Pardon me, Your Majesty," Rambling Richard said, "but that is the funniest thing I ever heard. You can't begin a story with 'Twice upon a time.'"

"You can't, can't you?" roared the king. "Where are my guards? To the jail with him! And don't let him out until he writes a story beginning 'Twice upon a time!'"

The guards dragged Rambling Richard off to the jail. That night, he laughed himself to sleep. But when he awoke in the morning, he did not feel like laughing. He knew that if he did not do as the king said, he would spend the rest of his life in jail.

His ink pot, his bundle of paper, and an extra goose quill pen were brought to him. He tried to write a story beginning "Twice upon a time," but he couldn't. The only way he could begin a story was "Once upon a time."

Every day the king's messenger came and asked if he was ready to read his story to the king. Every day Rambling Richard answered No. And every day he could hear the top of the mountain falling off with a BOOM, and the hole falling in with a ZOOM.

Rambling Richard began to think. He thought hard and long. And one day he said to the king's messenger, "Take me to the king."

"Ah," said the king's messenger. "You must be ready to read your story. Follow me to the palace."

Soon Rambling Richard was standing before the king.

"Well," said the king, "are you ready to read your story?"

"I am not," said Rambling Richard. "I cannot write a story that begins 'Twice upon a time.'"

"Back to the jail with him!" shouted the king. "Feed him nothing but bread and water! Guards! Back to the jail with him!"

"Just as you say, Your Majesty," said Rambling Richard. "But first let me tell you why I cannot write a story beginning 'Twice upon a time.'"

"And why is that?" asked the king.

Rambling Richard answered, "You say I must begin my story with 'Twice upon a time' because in Gib-Gib everything is twice as big, and you have two of anything anyone else has one of."

"Exactly," said the king.

"But it's not true," said Rambling Richard.

"What?" roared the king. "How so?"

"You have only one king," said Rambling Richard. "Why not two kings?"

The king leaned forward. "Did you say two kings?" he whispered.

"Two kings," said Rambling Richard.

"Two kings!" cried the soldiers, servants, and the king's uncles, cousins, and aunts.

"Guards! Clear the room!" ordered the king.

The guards cleared the room, and the king got down from his throne. He walked up and down, up and down. All day he walked up and down, and at first his face was red with rage, and then it was pale with worry.

At last he sent for Rambling Richard.

"What am I going to do?" he said. "I am the only king of
Gib-Gib. There isn't any other. And even if I could get an-
other one, what would I do with him? We would always be
getting in each other's way. Gib-Gib would be ruined."

He looked out the window. The top of the mountain was
falling off with a BOOM, and the hole was falling in with a
ZOOM.

"I wanted to be a great king," he said. "I wanted to be

the greatest king in the world. That's why I wanted two of anything anyone else has one of."

"That's no way to be a great king," said Rambling Richard. "It doesn't matter how big anything is, or how much or how many. If you want to be a great king, make your people happy."

"You know, I never thought of that," said the king.

"Then do so," said Rambling Richard sternly.

And the king did. He gave orders to stop work on the mountain. The hole was made into a swimming pool. One of the palaces was made into a school. All the signs were torn down and chopped into firewood.

Then the king invited everyone in Gib-Gib to a party. He sat on his throne, watching the people laughing and dancing and eating. After a while, he held up his hand for silence.

"Rambling Richard will now read a story," he said.

Rambling Richard stood next to the king. He cleared his throat, and began: "Once upon a time, in the kingdom of Gib-Gib . . ."

It was a long story, and a good story. When Rambling Richard finished reading it, everyone shouted and cheered.

The king said, "Rambling Richard, here is a bag of gold for you. I would like you to stay in Gib-Gib and write stories for me, for your story is twice as long as any I ever heard, and in Gib-Gib . . ."

Rambling Richard looked sharply at him.

"I'm sorry," said the king. "I forgot. Excuse me. It won't happen again. All the same, I would like you to stay."

"Thank you, Your Majesty," said Rambling Richard. "But I cannot do that. I must wander the world, writing stories and poems about everything I see."

The next day Rambling Richard bought a new hat and a purple cloak with extra-large pockets. He stuffed the pockets with stories and poems. He stuck his goose quill pen in his hat and picked up his ink pot and a bundle of paper.

He said good-bye, to the king, who walked with him to the gate of the city. A crowd of people followed, cheering and wishing him luck.

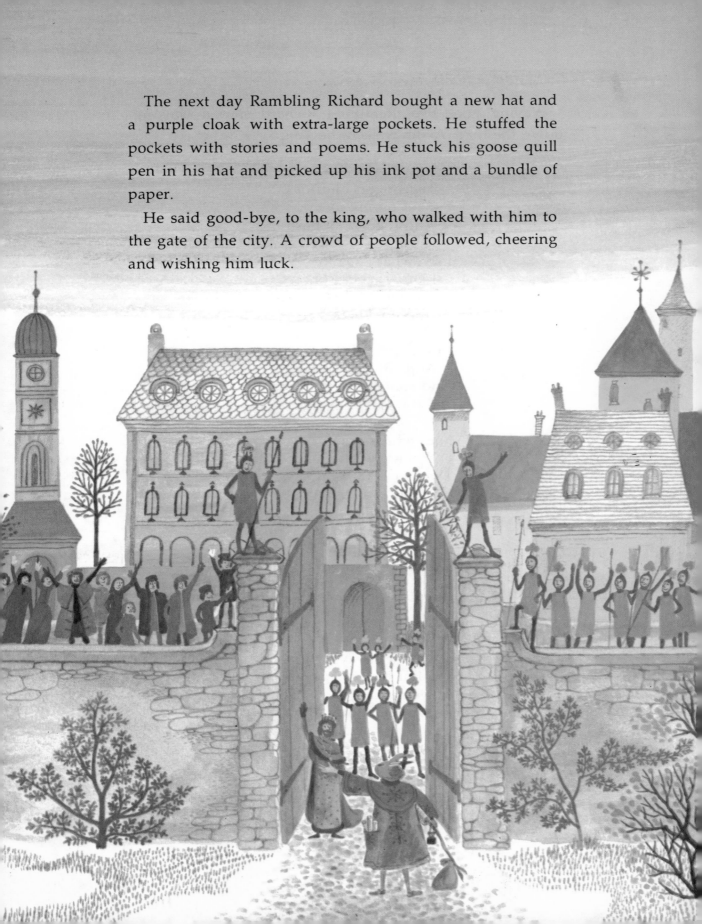

Waving good-bye, Rambling Richard started walking down the road. As he walked, he sang:

> I've two eyes and ears,
>   Ten fingers and toes,
> I stand on my feet,
>   And follow my nose.
>
> I see what I see,
>   I know what I know,
> I hear what I hear,
>   And go where I go.
>
> I think what I think,
>   And say what I say,
> And sometimes I'm sad,
>   But mostly I'm gay.
>
> I am what I am,
>   You are what you are,
> The sun is the sun,
>   A star is a star.
>
> Sometimes it's day,
>   And sometimes it's night,
> Sometimes I'm wrong,
>   But mostly I'm right.

And then he added, for good measure:

> It's not always true,
>   But as a rule,
> Even a king
>   Is sometimes a fool.